Pirates Ahoy!

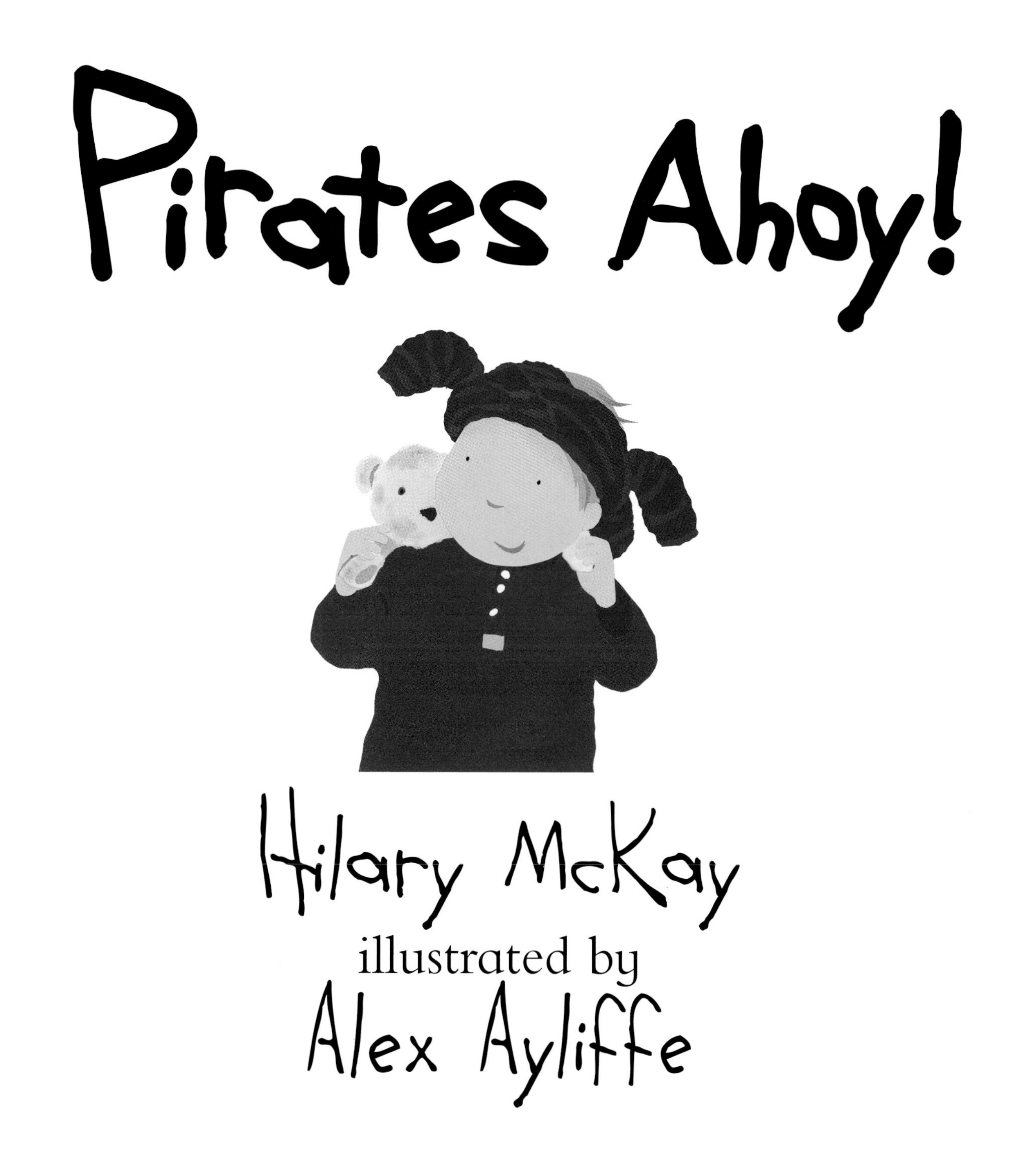

Hilary McKay
illustrated by
Alex Ayliffe

Margaret K. McElderry Books

To Jim and Snowy and Bella and Horlicks
—H. M.

For Peter and Lucie

—A. A.

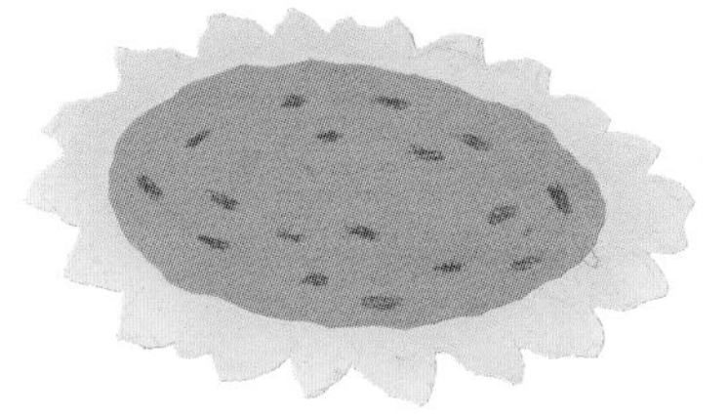

Margaret K. McElderry Books
An imprint of Simon & Schuster Children's Publishing Division
1230 Avenue of the Americas
New York, New York 10020

First published in London by Hodder Children's Books, a division of
Hodder Headline plc.

First United States Edition, 2000
10 9 8 7 6 5 4 3 2 1
Printed in Hong Kong

Library of Congress Catalog Card Number: 99-60169
ISBN: 0-689-83114-5

Once there were two boys
whose names were Simon and Peter.
Simon was three, and Peter was six.

Simon went to playgroup, but Peter went to Big School. Simon had brown hair, but Peter had bright red hair. Peter also had bright green eyes and 167 freckles that he said he had counted.

Simon's most favorite thing was Snowtop, his bear. Peter's most favorite thing was a secret. It wasn't his pop-up tent or his flashing-light sneakers.

"Floppy Bunny?" guessed Simon, thinking of his own lovely Snowtop.

"Floppy Bunny!' said Peter. "I don't play with baby things like Floppy Bunny anymore!"

Simon and Peter were cousins, so they shared the same grandmother. Gran lived in a quiet little bungalow and knitted sweaters for the boys.

One day Simon and Peter were sent to stay with Gran for a whole day and night. Their mothers said it would be nice.

"I'm not scared," said Simon, packing Snowtop, his most favorite thing.

Peter was not scared either, but he did not want to go. It wouldn't be any fun, he said. First he wouldn't get into the car and then he wouldn't get out of the car, but he ended up at Gran's anyway.

"Say hello to Simon and Snowtop, Peter!" said Gran.
"I don't play with baby things," said Peter.
"Say hello to Peter!" said Gran to Simon and Snowtop.
Simon and Snowtop did not say anything.
"Oh, well," said Gran. "I shall
get on with my knitting!"
And she went indoors.

When Gran had gone in, Peter sat on the kitchen step and made fierce grumbling noises. Simon poked him gently with his volcano-poking machine. Right away the noises grew louder and fiercer. Simon thought perhaps he would not play volcanoes after all.

"A jungle would be safer," he said to Snowtop, and they made one from two apple trees, the pole that propped up the clothesline, and three sunflower lions.

Then they were monkeys hanging from the clothesline pole. The pole sagged a bit.

A few minutes later Peter came into the jungle. He looked at Snowtop and didn't say anything, but when the lions attacked, Peter turned into a monkey, too. Simon wrestled with two lions to save Snowtop. Peter wrestled with his own lion.

But the lions were too fierce for Simon and Peter.

“To the beach! To the beach!” cried Simon. He tied his shirt around his head and turned into a pirate.

They built a pirate ship out of kitchen chairs, tea towels, the clothesline pole, and a bucket with Snowtop in it.
Peter started to look very cheerful, but then a terrible storm began.

The kitchen chairs capsized almost at once.
The mast and sails were blown away, and the bucket
with Snowtop plunged into the sea. Simon and Peter dived
in after him.

The sea was full of octopuses, disguised as Gran's nighties,
and stingrays, disguised as Gran's sweaters,
and sharks, disguised as Gran's underwear.
Luckily Snowtop turned into a great whale
and led them to a treasure island.

For a while on the island they were safe.
A kind lady with twinkling eyes brought
them sandwiches and potato chips
and apple pie and a sweater she
had knitted for Snowtop out of
leftover wool.

The sweater fitted Snowtop perfectly.
"Have you any more leftover wool?" asked Peter.
"I might have," said Gran.

After the pirate feast a strong wind blew up, and dinosaurs came out of the bushes. At first Peter fended off the dinosaurs with stalks of rhubarb.

Then there was no more rhubarb, and they had to flee for their lives.

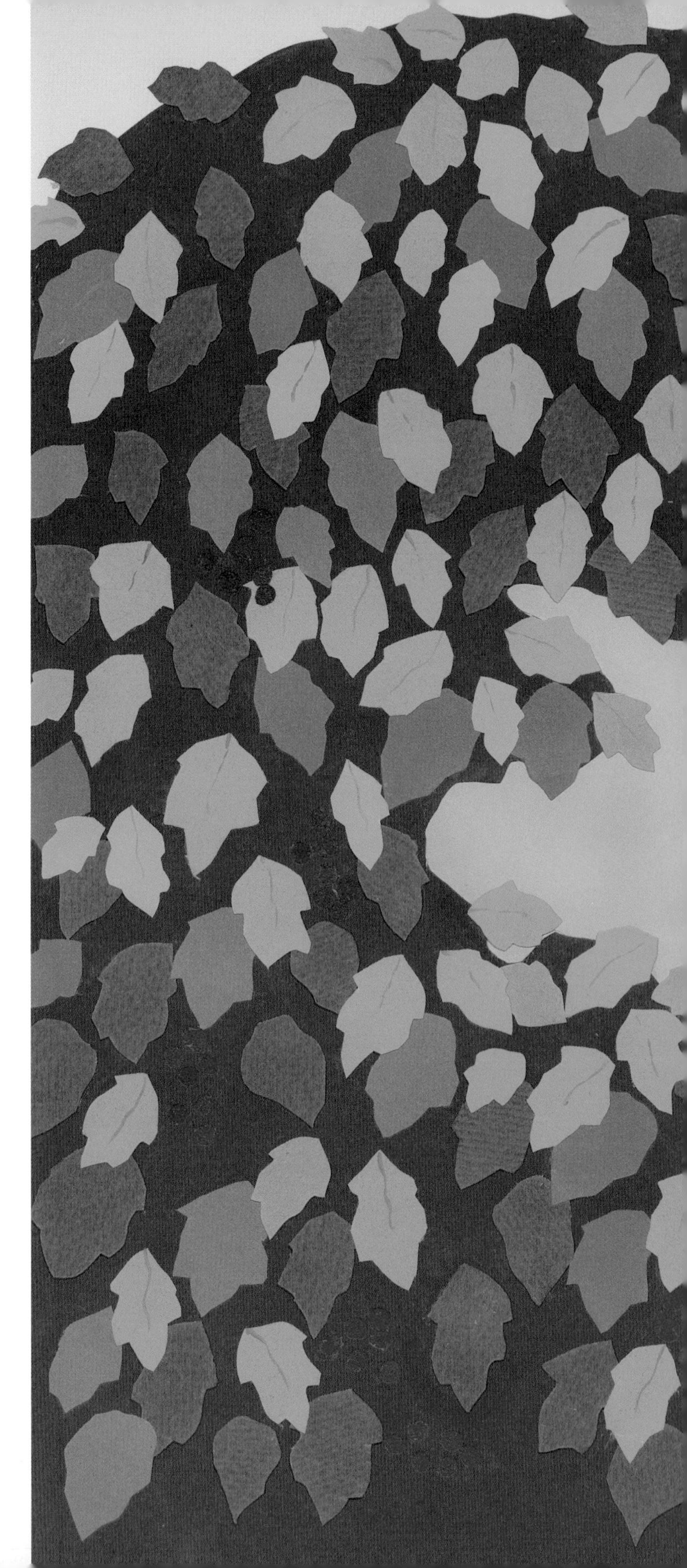

Night was coming, and the jungle was full of lions. The ship was wrecked. The sea seethed with sharks and stingrays and octopuses, and the island echoed with dinosaurs.

"Run to the vampire castle!" shouted Peter. "Quick!"

Luckily the vampire castle had a wide-open window. Peter boosted Simon over the windowsill and flung Snowtop after him. Then he climbed in himself.

There was a dressing table in the room loaded with vampire equipment. Snowtop grew fangs that glittered like diamonds. Simon and Peter dripped lipstick blood. They drew black stitches on their heads and turned their noses blue.

But, suddenly . . .

. . . lightning flashed across the room.
A wild woman came shrieking
through the doorway.
Streams of knitting trailed behind her.
She shouted,

"BED!"

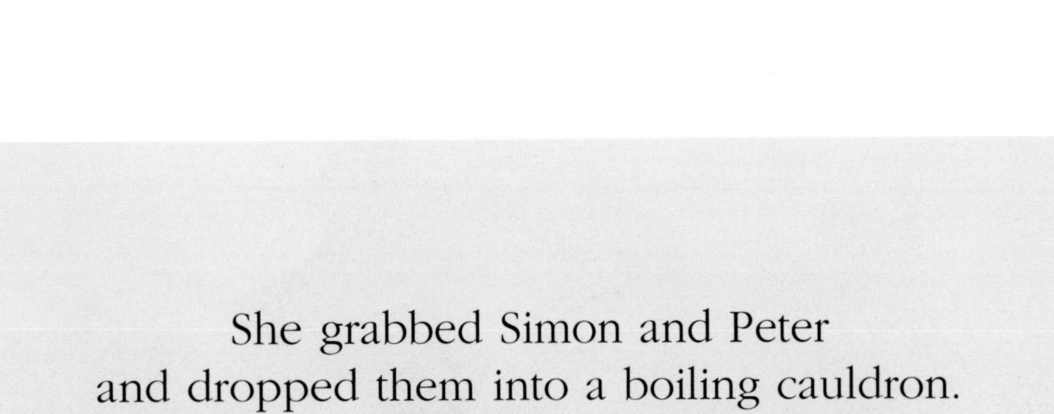

She grabbed Simon and Peter
and dropped them into a boiling cauldron.
She pulled out the third vampire's teeth.
"Careful!" said Simon and Peter.

The wild woman took no notice. They were scrubbed and rubbed and abandoned on two icebergs in the middle of the Arctic Ocean.

They crawled under the snow that covered their icebergs and wondered what she would do next. They were very relieved when she came tiptoeing in and they saw she had magically turned back into Gran.

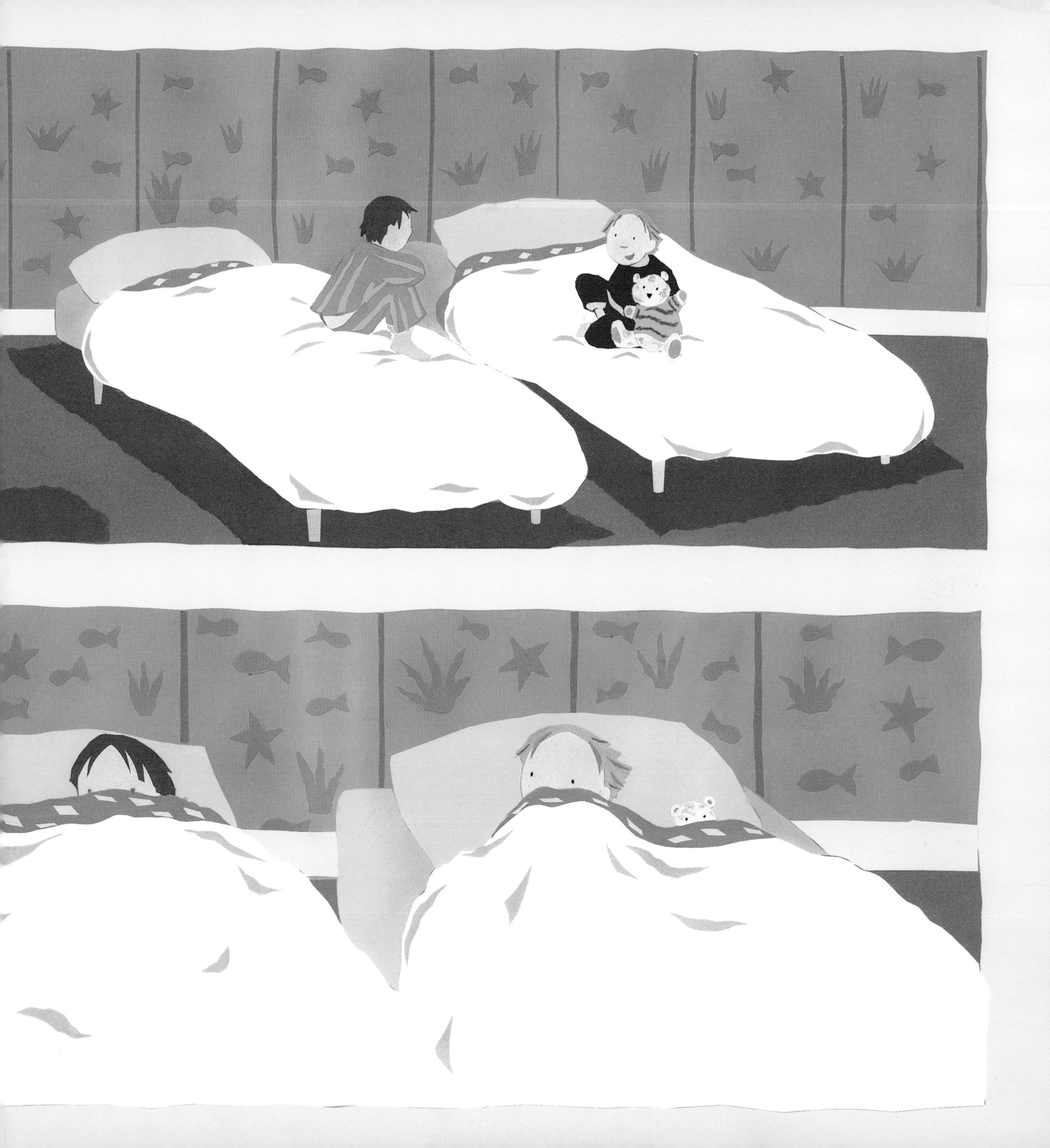

Gran tucked something under Peter's quilt that made a bump.
"There was *just* enough wool," Simon heard her whisper to Peter.
Peter reached up and grabbed the bump as if it was his very
most favorite thing.

Then Gran kissed them both, hugged them tight,
and left them together in the dark.
"Night-night, Peter," said Simon, snuggling down with Snowtop.
"Night, Simon," said Peter, snuggling down with the bump.
Then at last Simon guessed, and Peter's secret most favorite
thing was not a mystery anymore.

“Night, night, Floppy Bunny!” whispered Simon, very happily, across to the bump.

“Night, Snowtop,” said Peter.